The
Honey
and Bear
Stories

Stories by
URSULA DUBOSARSKY
—— Pictures by ——
RON BROOKS

PUFFIN BOOKS

*For Dover, who didn't have a book with his name in it,
so I wrote this one especially for him. x x x   U.D.*

For Hedwig and Griselda and Sally and Noel, good friends all.   R.B.

PUFFIN BOOKS

Published by the Penguin Group
Melbourne • London • New York • Ontario • Dublin
New Delhi • Auckland • Johannesburg
Penguin Books Ltd, Registered Offices: 80 Strand, London WC2R 0RL, England
Published by Penguin Group (Australia), 2010
1 3 5 7 9 10 8 6 4 2

Printed and bound in China by Everbest Printing Co. Ltd
National Library of Australia Cataloguing-in-Publication data available.
ISBN: 978 0 14 330500 2 (pbk.)

First published as *Honey and Bear* (1998) and
Special Days with Honey and Bear (2002)
by Penguin Books Australia Ltd.
This compilation published by Penguin Group (Australia), 2010.

Contents

Good Idea,
Bad Idea

One day, Bear had two ideas.

The first idea was to clean up
the kitchen.

Bear put on his apron and a pair of
yellow gloves. He didn't want his fur
to get dirty. Bear had beautiful fur.

He picked up a cloth and cleaned
the kitchen. He wiped the table.
He washed the dishes. He swept the
floor with a hairy broom.

Then he took off his apron and his gloves and sat down in his special armchair. He was very tired.
But the kitchen was lovely and clean!

Then Bear had the second idea.

'Honey will be home soon. I will cook her a seedy cake.'

Honey was a bird, and she liked seedy cakes.

So Bear went back to the kitchen. He mixed up the flour and the sugar and the butter and the eggs and lots and lots of black seeds in a bowl.

He poured it all into a tin, and put
the tin in the oven.

Just as the cake was ready, Honey
flew in the kitchen window.

'Hello Bear,' she said.

'Hello Honey,' said Bear.

Honey looked at the table. It was covered with eggshells. She looked in the sink. It was full of dirty dishes. She looked at the floor. There was flour all over it.

'What a mess!' said Honey.

'I know,' said Bear sadly.
'This morning I had an idea, to clean up the kitchen.'

'That was a good idea,' said Honey.

'Then I had a bad idea,' Bear went on. 'To cook you a cake. Now everything is a mess again.'

Honey looked in the oven.
'Oh!' she cried. 'Seedy cake!'

Bear took out the seedy cake and
put it on a plate. Bear ate the cake
with his big paws, and Honey pecked
at it with her beak.

After a little while, Honey said,
'I don't think it was a bad idea to make
the seedy cake, Bear.'

'No,' said Bear, licking his paws.
'Neither do I.'

Bear was thinking.

'You know,' he said, 'I did not have
a good idea and a bad idea. I had two
good ideas. I just had them in the
wrong order.'

'Yes!' said Honey. 'I see what you
mean, Bear.'

'Yes,' said Bear.

Bear and Honey looked at the empty
plate in front of them.

'I think I will make another seedy
cake now,' Bear said.
'Good idea!' said Honey.

Bear's Secret

One day, Bear did something bad.

He did the bad thing while Honey was sitting in the garden.

Bear took his bag of marbles, and dropped them one by one down the plug hole of the kitchen sink. This was very bad, but he kept doing it until all the marbles were gone.

'Oh, dear!' said Bear.

Honey came in the back door.

'What is it, Bear?' she asked.

'Oh, nothing!' said Bear, quickly, hiding the empty marble bag.

Honey poured herself a long glass of water. Some of it spilled into the sink.

'That's very strange,' she said. 'The water will not go down the plug hole.'

'Won't it?' said Bear.

'No,' said Honey, peering down. 'There must be something stuck down there.'

'I just remembered,' said Bear, suddenly. 'I must go out into the garden right now to do some digging.'

But Honey did not seem to hear. She was inside the sink, looking down the plug hole.

Out in the garden,
Bear picked up a spade
and dug in the dirt.
He took the hose
and poured water
all over the earth
until it turned into
mud. Then he dug
some more.

'Bear!' Honey called out from the
kitchen window.

'I can't come now!' Bear called back.
'I'm far too dirty!' He held up his paws.

'Just come to the window, Bear,' said
Honey, 'and look at what I found down
the plug hole.'

On the window-sill was a big bowl
of marbles.

'Ah,' said Bear. 'How did you get
them out?'

'I can make my neck quite long
when I need to,' replied Honey. 'And
I have my beak, you know.'

'Oh, well,' said Bear, looking down
at the ground. 'I have to go back to my
digging now.'

Later, when Honey was reading,
Bear went into the kitchen and took
out the marble bag from where he
had hidden it. One by one, he put
all the marbles from the bowl back
into the bag.

Bear never told Honey that he was the one who dropped the marbles down the plug hole.

Bear never told anyone at all.

It was his secret.

Counting Leaves

Honey was bored.

Bear was fast asleep in his special armchair, and Honey had no one to talk to and nothing to do.

'Why does Bear have to sleep so much,' she wondered. 'I hardly sleep at all. It's so boring for me when Bear is asleep.'

She looked out the window – how cold it must be out there!

All the leaves were falling, like
snowflakes, from the trees into the lake.

'I know!' said Honey suddenly.

'I will count the leaves that fall from the trees outside – that will help the time to pass!'

She sat herself on the window-sill and laid her beak against the glass. It wasn't very comfortable, but it was the best spot to sit for counting.

'One, two, three, four,' began Honey. 'Five, six, seven, eight,' she went on.

Honey counted and counted.

The leaves fell and Honey kept counting. Bear began to snore, but she didn't hear him.

She forgot about not being comfortable.

She forgot about being bored.

All she wanted to do was count those leaves.

The sun began to set, and it got colder and darker and it was hard to see, but Honey kept on counting.

'Nine million, six-hundred-and-two-thousand, two-hundred-and-three,' said Honey at last. And Bear woke up.

'What did you say?' he asked with a big bear's yawn.

Honey turned around. 'Bear!' she said. 'It's you!'

'So it is!' replied Bear, surprised. 'I've been asleep.'

'Yes, you have,' said Honey. 'For such a long time.'

'What have you been doing with yourself, then?' asked Bear.

Honey looked out the window.

Down fell the leaves in the wind, one after the other. Millions and millions of leaves.

'Oh, nothing really,' she said. 'Just waiting for you to wake up, Bear.'

The Visit

Bear and Honey were going on a visit.

They were going to see Bear's mother, who lived on the other side of the lake. Bear had not seen his mother for a long time.

'Let's take some sandwiches and some orange juice,' said Honey, 'and we can have a picnic on the way.'

'Yes,' agreed Bear, 'and a couple of nice bananas.' Bear loved bananas.

Honey made sandwiches with
chocolate spread and put them in a
backpack for Bear to carry. It was a
warm day, just right for a walk.

Bear hummed as he walked along, while Honey flew above his head.

'I am making up a song for my mother,' said Bear, 'so I have something to sing when I see her.'

Bear and Honey made their way around the edge of the lake. Sometimes Honey flew on ahead and waited for Bear in the branches of a tree.

When they were halfway around,
Bear called out to Honey, 'Let's stop
here and eat half our lunch!'

So they sat down and ate half the
sandwiches and drank half the juice
and shared one banana.

'Off we go again,' said Bear, standing up. He had some grass stains on his fur, but Honey didn't like to say anything. She didn't think Bear's mother would mind.

When they had walked a bit further, Bear called out to Honey, 'Let's stop here and eat the other half of our lunch!'

So they sat down on a pile of pebbles near the edge of the water and ate the rest of the sandwiches and drank the rest of the juice. Bear ate the second banana all by himself, because Honey wasn't hungry anymore.

'Well, off we go again,' said Bear, standing up.

Honey noticed that Bear now had some pebble stains on his fur as well as grass stains, but she still didn't say anything.

'How is the song going, Bear?' she asked instead, as she flew in a circle above his humming. 'Oh, pretty well,' replied Bear, smiling to himself.

They came right around the lake,
to the place where Bear's mother lived
and where Bear himself had lived
when he was a tiny bear cub.

On the door of the house was a note.

Bear was quiet.

'She must have a lot of visiting to
do,' said Honey. 'Three weeks!'

'Yes,' said Bear.

'You could write a message on the bottom of the paper,' suggested Honey, 'to let her know we've been by.'

Bear thought for a moment.

'But if I do that, Honey, my mother will be sad that she missed us. If I don't write anything, she'll never know we were here, so she won't be sad.'

'Yes, I see what you mean, Bear,' said Honey.

On the way back, Bear sang Honey the song he had made up for his mother. There weren't any words, just a lot of humming.

'Ummmmmmmmmmmmm,' sang Bear.

When they reached their own house it was night-time.

'Look, Honey,' said Bear. 'I am dirty from the grass and the pebbles. I must have a wash.'

He fetched a bucket to fill the bath. When there was enough water, he stepped in. Honey perched on the back of a chair. She did not like to get her feathers wet.

'Anyway, we had a lovely picnic,' said Bear, scrubbing himself. 'And maybe next time we visit, my mother will be at home!'

'I'm sure she will, Bear,' agreed Honey.

Honey is Cross

Honey was cross.

She was cross all day.

'Why are you cross?' asked Bear.

'Oh, I don't know!' snapped Honey.

'Will you play a game with me?' asked Bear, holding up a box of cards.

'No,' said Honey. 'I don't want to play any games. I'm going out.'

'But Honey!' said Bear. 'It's nearly dinner time and we are having peas!'

Peas was Honey's favourite dinner.
But she flapped her wings at Bear.

'I'm not hungry. I'm sick of peas
and I'm sick of games. I'm going to fly
away somewhere.'

Up she flew, into the air and out the kitchen window. She did not even look back at Bear, she was so cross.

Honey flew and flew. She flapped her wings, going faster and higher. She flew further than she had ever been in her life, she was so cross.

She flew far away from the lake and the trees and far away from Bear.

'I am very high in the sky!' thought
Honey. 'I am higher than I have
ever been.'

Honey began to feel tired. In the
distance she saw a mountain.

'I will stop there,' she said to herself.

When Honey reached the mountain,
she fluttered down on a rocky ledge.

'Hello, bird,' said a voice.

Honey turned and saw an eagle.

'Oh,' said Honey, feeling weak.
'Hello.'

'How nice to meet you,' said the eagle.

How big he was! He had a strong, round beak and dark, shiny feathers. Honey had never seen such a wonderful bird so close.

'Is this where you live?' she asked.

'Sometimes,' replied the eagle.
'I move about a bit, you know.'

'Do you?' said Honey. 'I would like that, I think. Then I would not get so bored.'

'I never get bored!' said the eagle.
'There is too much to do.'

Up came the wind, over the
mountain top. Honey hung on tight.

'What do you do?' she asked.

Suddenly, the eagle lifted his huge
wings. He gazed down at the ground
way below. Something was moving,
a rabbit or a mouse. He raised a claw
up into the air.

Honey shivered.

'Are you frightened?' asked the eagle.

'No.' Honey shook her head. 'It's just
the shadow of your wings. It makes me
feel cold.'

'I have to go now,' said the eagle.
'I'm hungry. Perhaps I will see you
later on.'

'Perhaps,' said Honey. 'Goodbye.'

When the eagle had
gone, Honey spread
out her own wings.
They made only a tiny shadow.
She moved her own little beak
up and down.
Honey did not need
a big sharp beak
or spiky claws
to eat seeds.
Or peas.

    She flew off the mountain and away.
She flew and flew, flapping her wings
harder and harder, until she came
all the way back to the house, and to
Bear.

    Bear was sitting at the table with a
plate of peas.

'Oh, Bear!' cried Honey, as she came in though the window. 'Are there any peas left?'

'Of course there are,' he said. 'Only they are not so warm now, you know.'

After Honey finished her peas, she
sat with Bear in his special armchair.

'You fur is so soft and warm, Bear,'
said Honey.

'Are you still cross?' asked Bear.

'No,' replied Honey, falling asleep.
She had flown such a long, long way.

'Not anymore, Bear.'

Staying Up Late

Honey and Bear were sitting in the kitchen eating apples.

'Bear,' said Honey, 'today is a very special day.'

'Is it?' said Bear, his mouth full.

'Yes,' said Honey. 'Today is the last day of the year.'

'Oh,' said Bear.

'So do you know what we have to do tonight?' said Honey.

'What?' asked Bear, excited.

'We have to stay up till the middle of the night and look at the clock,' said Honey.

'That doesn't sound very interesting,' said Bear.

'But it is, Bear,' said Honey. 'We will look at the clock, and when both hands are on the twelve, it will be the New Year! Then we will give each other a kiss.'

Bear thought for a moment. 'I could give you a kiss now,' he said, 'in case I am too tired in the middle of the night.'

'No, Bear,' said Honey. 'We have to wait until twelve o'clock.'

When they had finished the apples, Honey and Bear went outside. They went for a long, long walk by the lake until the sun was setting.

By the time they got home, it was
night.

Bear sat in his armchair and looked
at the clock.

Nine o'clock. He yawned. He was
already tired. How would he stay up
until twelve o'clock?

'Let's do a jigsaw,' said Honey.

So they sat on the floor and began a jigsaw. It was hard. After a while, Bear stood up and looked at the clock. Ten o'clock.

Oh dear, he thought.

'Bear, can you see where this piece goes?' asked Honey.

Bear sat down.

The clock ticked.

Bear yawned.

Eleven o'clock.

'Let's go to sleep, Honey,' Bear said.
'Please?'

But Honey was busy with the puzzle.

Bear sighed.

He picked up a piece and tried to fit
it in. But he was just too tired.

At last, Bear couldn't wait any longer.

'Honey,' he said. 'I *have* to go to bed!'

'But Bear! Look! Look at the clock!'
Honey shouted, flapping her wings.

Bear looked.
The little hand
was on the twelve,
and the big
hand was
nearly there.

'It's almost the New Year!'
said Bear.

Honey and Bear
held their breath.

They waited. They watched.

The big hand moved such
a tiny bit and –

'HAPPY NEW YEAR!' cried
Honey and Bear at the same time.
They forgot all about the puzzle, and
gave each other a big kiss.

They went and opened the front
door. Bear gazed up at the sky and
the stars and the moon of the bright
new year.

'Honey, look!' said Bear softly.

But he was whispering to himself.
Honey was fast asleep. She had closed
her eyes, and did not open them again
until the sun came up in the morning.

The Mirror

One day, Bear was digging in the garden. He found something, flat and round and shiny. Bear lifted it up with his spade. He took it in his paw and shook off the dirt.

'Honey!' he called. 'Look what I've found!'

Honey flew down onto Bear's shoulder. She stretched out her neck and looked into the shiny circle.

'Bear!' she said. 'It's me!'

Bear peered in. 'No it's not, Honey,'
he said. 'It's me.'

Honey and Bear stared at each
other, and at the circle again.

'Bear,' said Honey, 'it's both of us.'

'Except,' said Bear slowly,
'we're backwards.'

Suddenly, Bear felt frightened. He
did not want to see himself backwards.

'Put it away, Honey,' he said. 'We
don't need it.'

'But it's so useful!' said Honey.
'If I look into it, I can see if a little bit
of spaghetti is hanging out of my beak.'

'I could tell you that,' said Bear.
'If you like.'

'It's not the same as seeing it for
yourself, Bear,' replied Honey.

Honey was very pleased with what
Bear had found in the garden.

She washed it in the sink and dried
it in the sun. Then she hung it on a nail
just inside the front door.

She looked into it again, with her
head on one side. She looked at her
eyes and at the silver in her wings.

'I won't look at it, ever!' declared
Bear, watching her.

Later that day, Bear passed by the shiny circle.

He stopped, just for a moment.

He blinked. 'Hello, Bear!' he said out loud. Then he ran as fast as he could out the door and over to the sandpit under the lemon tree.

'Actually,' he said, wriggling his toes in the sand, 'I'm a rather nice-looking Bear!'

Bear's Birthday

It was Bear's birthday.

He was in the garden, standing upside-down on his head.

'Bear,' said Honey, 'what are you doing?'

'Today is my birthday,' said Bear. 'Remember? That means I can do whatever I want. And I want to stand on my head. Look at me!'

Honey looked. She wished she could
stand on her head.

Bear turned the right way up.

'Now I want to do something else,' he said.

'What?' asked Honey.

'Now I want to make a big noise!' said Bear. He pulled out a paper bag suddenly from his pocket.

He blew into the paper bag until it was full of air. Then he popped it – BANG! – with his paw.

'Ow!' said Honey.

'Now I want to play a game,' said Bear. 'Let's play riddles!'

'Oh, good,' said Honey. 'I like riddles.'

'What is big and round and starts with Mmmmmmmmmm?' said Bear.

Honey thought.

'A marble?'

'No,' said Bear.

'A mountain?'

'No,' said Bear.

'Give up?'

'A yellow balloon!' Bear laughed and jumped up and down.

'But Bear –' began Honey, 'that's not . . .'

'It was a tricky riddle, wasn't it?' said Bear. 'Do you want to hear another one?'

'No,' said Honey. She flew away
with a loud flap, high onto the roof.
'Honey?' said Bear, looking up.
'Come down and play with me.'

'I don't want to,' said Honey.

Bear stared. 'Honey,' he said, 'are you crying?'

Honey did not answer.

'It's not very nice of you to cry,' said Bear. 'You are spoiling my birthday.'

Bear sat down on the step. Honey sat up on the roof. They sat and they sat. And they sat. And they sat.

Finally, Bear stood up.

'Honey,' he said, 'would you like to help me blow out the candles on my birthday cake?'

Honey flew down from the roof.

'All right,' she said.

Bear brought out the cake. All the candles were alight.

Bear and Honey blew them out.
It took Honey a long time because her breath was so small, but there were no more tears.

Then Bear closed his eyes and made
a wish, because it was his birthday,
after all.

'What did you wish for, Bear?' asked
Honey.

'Just for everything!' said Bear.
'Just everything!'

Bear Gets Lost

Bear was always losing things.

He lost his hat.

He lost his pencils.

He was always losing his socks.

One day, Bear even lost himself.

It was a windy day. Bear loved the wind. He put on his big blue coat and his scarf and shouted, 'Goodbye, Honey! I am going out!'

Usually, Honey and Bear went out
walking together. But on this windy
day, Bear wanted to go out by himself.

He walked down to the lake.
He watched the wind pull the water
into waves, and the leaves fly about in
the sky. He opened his mouth and let
the air rush right inside him.

It made him laugh, and he started
to run.

He ran up and down with his arms
spread out.

He flopped down and lay still,
panting, with his eyes closed.

After a while, he sat up and looked
about. He was in a field of grass and
flowers, on top of a slope.

I wonder where I am? he thought.
Am I lost?

Bear rolled himself down the slope
like a rolling pin.

When he came to a stop, he felt dizzy all over. Bear laughed again. I can't be lost, he decided. I don't feel lost. If I were lost, I would feel sad. I would feel lonely. Perhaps I would cry.

But Bear was lost. When it was dark
and he still wasn't home, Honey came
looking for him. She flew far and wide,
with a little lantern around her neck.

At last she found him.

'Bear,' cried Honey. 'There you are!
Did you get lost?'

'I think I did,' said Bear.

Bear was glad that Honey had found
him. He was glad to follow her lantern
through the night all the way back to
their home.

But he often thought about the windy day when he lost himself. It made him feel happy to remember it.

It was a special day.

Honey's Dream

On Christmas Eve, Honey had the strangest dream.

She dreamed that she was a dove that belonged to a magician.

The magician had a black hat and a big black cape.

When it was time for the magic show to begin, he opened a cage. Honey flew out and perched on his sleeve.

'Abracadabra!' cried the magician.
'I will now make this bird disappear!'
He waved his magic wand. There
was a bang and a cloud of smoke.
Honey was gone!

She found herself on top of a very tall tree. It was the middle of the night. It was still and silent. There was only one star in the sky. The magician was nowhere to be seen, but Honey could feel magic all around her.

The star grew brighter and shone in Honey's eyes.

What is that sound? she wondered. She heard a rustling, like the beating of hundreds of wings.

She looked down to the ground far below. There were movements in the darkness, of animals and people. The star grew even brighter and a little wind rose.

[91]

Honey heard voices singing, then a tiny cry of something so very small.

'Oh,' Honey whispered, 'I must fly down and see what it is.'

And she leapt off the tree into the night.

Then Honey woke up. In her own
room. How her heart was thumping!
She stretched out her wings. They
were brown and small, not wide and
feathery-white. She was not a dove on
top of a huge tree. She was Honey.

Bear opened his eyes.

'What is it, Honey?' he asked.

'What's happened?'

'Oh, Bear,' said Honey, flying onto
his paw. 'Bear, it's Christmas Day.'

Ursula
and tale
internatio
literary aw
their univers
of small mom
young readers.

You can find out
ursuladubosarsky.com.

ABOUT THE

Ron Brooks is an award-winning
artist who has been illustrating ch
over thirty years. His work includes
classics as *The Bunyip of Berkeley's Creek* an   .n,
Rose and the Midnight Cat, both written   Jenny
Wagner, and *Old Pig* and *Fox*, by Margaret Wild.

Ron's tender and heartwarming pictures in the
Honey and Bear stories reflect his extraordinary
ability to explore emotion and character.